little Miss Trouble

by Roger Hargreaves

WORLD INTERNATIONAL

"Here comes trouble," people used to say.

And who do you think would come walking along?

That's right!

Little Miss Trouble.

Oh, the trouble she caused.

One morning she went to see Mr Uppity.

"Do you know what Mr Small calls you behind your back?" she asked him.

"No," replied Mr Uppity.

"What does Mr Small call me behind my back?"

Little Miss Trouble looked at him.

"Fatty!" she said.

Now, Mr Uppity didn't like that.

Not at all.

Not one little bit.

He went round immediately to see Mr Small.

"How dare you call me FATTY?" he shouted.

"But..." stammered Mr Small, who never had called him 'Fatty'.

"But..."

"But nothing," shouted Mr Uppity.

And he hit poor Mr Small.

Ouch!

And gave him a black eye.

Poor Mr Small.

Little Miss Trouble, who was hiding behind a tree, hugged herself with glee.

"Oh, I do so like making trouble," she giggled to herself.

Naughty girl!

Little Miss Trouble went to see Mr Clever.

"Do you know what Mr Small calls you behind your back?" she asked him.

"No," replied Mr Clever.

"Tell me! What does Mr Small call me behind my back?"

Little Miss Trouble looked at him.

"Big Nose!" she said.

Now.

Mr Clever didn't like that very much either.

Off he rushed.

And, when he found Mr Small, without waiting for an explanation, he punched him!

Hard!

In the other eye!

Poor Mr Small.

Two black eyes for something he'd never done.

"Oh look at you," Miss Trouble laughed when she saw him.

"It's all your fault," said Mr Small.

"True," she said.

And walked off.

Poor Mr Small had to go to the doctor.

"Good heavens!" exclaimed Doctor Makeyouwell when he saw him. "Whatever happened to you?"

Mr Small explained.

"I think," Doctor Makeyouwell said when he'd heard what Mr Small had to tell him, "that something should be done about that little lady! What she needs is..."

Then he stopped.

And he chuckled.

"That's it," he laughed.

"What's it?" asked Mr Small.

And Doctor Makeyouwell whispered something to Mr Small.

Would you like to know what he whispered?

Not telling you!

It's a secret!

That afternoon Mr Small went to see Mr Tickle.

"Do you know what Miss Trouble calls you behind your back?" he asked.

"No," said Mr Tickle.

"What does Miss Trouble call me behind my back?"

Mr Small looked at him.

"Pudding Face!" he said.

Then Mr Small went to see Mr Bump.

"Do you know what Miss Trouble calls you behind your back?" he asked.

"No," said Mr Bump.

"What does Miss Trouble call me behind my back?"

Mr Small looked at him.

"Mr Nitwit!" he said.

Little Miss Trouble was in trouble.

"How dare you call me 'Pudding Face'?" cried Mr Tickle.

And tickled her.

"And how dare you call me 'Mr Nitwit'?" cried Mr Bump.

And bumped her.

Now, I don't know whether you've ever been tickled and bumped at the same time, but it's not much fun.

In fact it's no fun at all.

Ticklebumpticklebumpticklebumpticklebump!

For ten minutes.

And ten minutes of ticklebumping is a long time.

I can tell you!

Later that evening Doctor Makeyouwell strolled round to see Mr Small.

"How are the eyes?" he asked.

"Oh much better now thank you," replied Mr Small.

"And did our little plan work?" asked the doctor.

"It did indeed," grinned Mr Small.

"Shake," said Doctor Makeyouwell.

And they shook hands.

Well.

Not quite hands.

Doctor Makeyouwell then strolled round to see Miss Trouble.

She was feeling very sorry for herself.

"What's wrong with you?" he asked her.

And she told him all about it.

All about everything.

Doctor Makeyouwell looked at her.

"Cheer up," he said.

"You know what you've just had, don't you?"

Little Miss Trouble shook her head.

"A taste of your own medicine," he chuckled.

And went home.

For supper.

Fantastic offers for Little Miss fans!

Collect all your Mr. Men or Little Miss books in these superb durable collectors' cases!

Only £5.99 inc. postage and packing, these wipe-clean, hard-wearing cases will give all your Mr. Men or Little Miss books a beautiful new home!

Keep track of your collection with this giant-sized double-sided Mr. Men and Little Miss Collectors' poster.

Collect 6 tokens and we will send you a brilliant giant-sized double-sided collectors' poster! Simply tape a £1 coin to cover postage and packaging in the space provided and fill out the form overleaf.

Only need a few Little Miss or Mr. Men to complete your set? You can order any of the titles on the back of the books from our Mr. Men order line on 0870 787 1724. Orders should be delivered between 5 and 7 working days.

--- **TO BE COMPLETED BY AN ADULT** ---

To apply for any of these great offers, ask an adult to complete the details below and send this whole page with the appropriate payment and tokens, to: MR. MEN CLASSIC OFFER, PO BOX 715, HORSHAM RH12 5WG

☐ Please send me a giant-sized double-sided collectors' poster.

AND ☐ I enclose 6 tokens and have taped a £1 coin to the other side of this page.

☐ Please send me ☐ Mr. Men Library case(s) and/or ☐ Little Miss library case(s) at £5.99 each inc P&P

☐ I enclose a cheque/postal order payable to Egmont UK Limited for £...............

OR ☐ Please debit my MasterCard / Visa / Maestro / Delta account (delete as appropriate) for £...............

Card no. ☐☐☐☐ ☐☐☐☐ ☐☐☐☐ ☐☐☐☐ ☐☐☐☐   Security code ☐☐☐

Issue no. (if available) ☐   Start Date ☐☐/☐☐/☐☐   Expiry Date ☐☐/☐☐/☐☐

Fan's name: ....   Date of birth: ....

Address: ....

....

Postcode: ....

Name of parent / guardian: ....

Email for parent / guardian: ....

Signature of parent / guardian: ....

Please allow 28 days for delivery. Offer is only available while stocks last. We reserve the right to change the terms of this offer at any time and we offer a 14 day money back guarantee. This does not affect your statutory rights. Offers apply to UK only.

☐ We may occasionally wish to send you information about other Egmont children's books. If you would rather we didn't, please tick this box.

Ref: LIM 001